DRAGON'S MASQUERADE
A DRAGONDELL HOLIDAY SHORT

DAWN MCGRAW

Copyright © 2019 by Dawn McGraw

All rights reserved.

No part of this book may be reproduced in any form or by any electronic or mechanical means, including information storage and retrieval systems, without written permission from the author, except for the use of brief quotations embodied in critical reviews and certain other noncommercial uses permitted by copyright law. For permission requests, please contact dawn@dawnmcgraw.com

This is a work of fiction. Names, characters, places and incidents are either the product of the author's imagination or are used fictitiously, and any resemblance to actual persons, living or dead, business establishments, events, or locales is entirely coincidental.

Cover Art: Z Designs

ALSO BY DAWN MCGRAW

Dragondell

Dragon's Second Chance
Dragon's Acquisition
Dragon's Rogue

Dragondell Holiday Short

Dragon's Masquerade
Dragon's Feast
Dragon's Yuletide Frenzy
Dragon's Countdown
Dragon's Heart

Dragon's Mate Holiday

Hoarding His Halloween
Treasuring His Thanksgiving
Claiming His Christmas

For my miracle babies...
May life bring an equal blessing to you.

ACKNOWLEDGMENTS

This short story would not be possible without many wonderful people who helped me find my way. Especially, Zoey Indiana. I'm so lucky to have found a friend with the same crazy dream. I wouldn't have done any of this without your support and camaraderie. Best writing partner ever!

I'd also like to thank the members of Colorado Romance Writers who have graciously pointed me in the proper direction, patiently suffering through my myriad questions. Jessica Aspen, Aidy Award, Alyssa Dean Copeland, M.L. Guida, Helen Hardt, Jean Jacobson, Liz Kelley, McKenna Rogue, just to name a few. You are my heros.

CONTENTS

Chapter 1	1
Chapter 2	5
Chapter 3	10
Chapter 4	14
Chapter 5	18
Chapter 6	22
Chapter 7	25
Chapter 8	29
Epilogue	36
Skunk Odor Neutralizer	46
Sneak peak of Dragon's Feast	47
A Note From the Author	55
About the Author	57

CHAPTER 1

Izzy stomped the snow from her boots onto the thick rug, mindful of the rustic wooden floor. Relief flooded her system, she'd been lucky to find shelter before the main thrust of the storm hit. After her car spun out into the ditch, she hadn't expected to catch a break. Then she saw the sign, *Fallbrook Wedding*, thankfully these people hadn't cancelled. The deposit on a huge place like this must be astronomical. Now, all she had to do was crash this wedding and everything would be a-okay. Hopefully, no one would notice her if she sat in the back. She tossed her jacket amongst the ones hanging near the door and slowly pulled the inner door open a crack.

Crap, this was some sort of costumed affair. The room was full of the most amazing cosplay costumes she'd ever seen. Frustration raced down her spine and kicked her feet into motion. Pacing back to the entrance, the door closed behind her with a soft click.. She'd never hide in that room without a costume, she'd be a blight on their role play atmosphere. Even in costume, they wore tuxes and gowns. A costume so realistic, let alone a dress that fancy, had never graced her closet.

She grabbed her jacket and stuffed her arms into the sleeves, then flung open the door and stared out into a white wall of snow. Wow, this safe haven had appeared at just the right time. No way could she go back out in that.

"Excuse me." A voice as chilly as the storm pricked her neck.

Izzy cringed.

Busted.

FARRYN CAUGHT SIGHT OF AGGIRON, JUST THE DRAGON HE WAS looking for. He excused himself from the conversation he was in and followed after the head of the elite team. They had been hand picked by the head of the council himself. Now that was a group of dragons to get in good with. He wondered how to introduce himself while struggling to intercept Aggiron at the cathedral windows. What did you get a group of dragons who had everything? Somehow he would figure it out and be the solution the team didn't even know they needed. He'd nearly caught up when he noticed Aggiron was moving quickly toward the kitchen dragging a frightened little human behind him. She wasn't in costume, so must be a member of the staff. From the looks of it, she was going to get a dressing down. What a sad way to spend your Halloween.

As he approached the kitchen doors, he decided he should remain outside and let the poor woman save face. He leaned against the two story rustic beam holding up the ceiling. A delicious spiced orange cider scent tumbled from the swinging staff doors, it smelled exactly like his favorite wassail. Unfortunately, it was undercut by the acrid stench of the women's fear. So he wouldn't add to her distress, he shifted into human form. Maybe he should step inside and make sure she was alright.

Izzy stared at the big oaf of a dragon. She'd seen cosplay online, but never realized it could be so realistic, like on a Hollywood set. He didn't look crazy, but obviously looks were deceiving. "You can't be serious."

"Indeed, I am. It's the safest place for you." He held the kitchen pantry door open and had the nerve to act like she was wasting his time.

"I'm not going to interrupt your fancy shindig, I'll just stay out of the way and keep warm."

"Yes, out of the way. Exactly." He waived her in again and huffed loudly when she crossed her arms and shook her head. "Look, I don't have time to babysit you all night, so for fates sake, get in the pantry."

"Look, I didn't intend to crash your super important role playing event, I had an accident. Let me call a tow truck and I'll be on my way as soon as they get here." Idiot men were going to be the death of her. Her nincompoop coworker, Eric, started it with the office ski trip from hell. As if she didn't hate her job enough as it was. She could kick herself for leaving her stupid charger in the hotel. Unfortunately she just couldn't seem to catch a break since. There was no way she was letting this idiot lock her in a damn closet.

He scratched his arm, roughly like he was having a bad allergic reaction to his costume and was trying to scrape off the top layer of his skin. Then spit into his hand. *Gross!* "I'm not wasting any more time with you." He reached for her arm, but missed.

She dodged behind the large stainless steel island and

backed away quickly, arms out wide trying to calm him. "Let's be reasonable. Call the sheriff or a tow truck, but I'm not being locked in a closet." This was ludicrous. She might not like her life, but she didn't want it to end in a pantry.

When she backed into a warm wall of muscle, icy fear froze her system. This couldn't be good. Humongous hands gripped her upper arms stopping her in her tracks and giving her a nasty static shock. "Perhaps I can be of service." Rumbled from behind her.

Crap. Now what?

CHAPTER 2

Farryn's fingers thrummed from the electrical current cascading through him as he gripped the woman's delicate arms, but suppressed his reaction. It was a simple static shock, there was no way his mating response was kicking in. Not when he had so much riding on this event. He'd caught enough of the conversation to understand the situation. She was stranded here and Aggiron needed to get back to the festivities. Exactly the kind of opportunity he'd been looking for.

"She's not part of the humans that belong here." Aggiron stepped forward to take her, and she tried to duck under Ferryn's arm. Shifting positions, he pulled her into his side and hugged her close. Pinning her against him.

"I can keep track of her for you." He'd seen the weather, there wasn't a chance in hell that a tow truck was getting here this evening. Even if expedient, locking her up would only lead to more complications, someone had to guard her.

"All I need is a phone or a charger and I'll take care of myself." She tried again to pull away from him. Everywhere her body touched was twitching and that delicious orange spice scent of hers was getting all over him. He hadn't been this close to a woman in years, hadn't wanted to bother. But he needed to be useful to the dragon in front of him, no matter what it took.

"Why don't I know you?" Aggiron kept his eyes glued to the woman, like he expected her to make some sort of huge scene at any moment.

"I'm Farryn, I recently accepted the council's invitation." So many had heeded the summons, that Dragondell was now stock full. Probably half the entire population of dragons lived there or in the surrounding area. After a hundred years on his own, it was like returning home to find your favorite robe no longer fit.

"Pleasure to meet you Farryn, I'm Izzy. Could you please let me go?"

Aggiron clapped his hands together and spoke a spell so quietly the human probably couldn't hear. All their senses were less acute than a dragon's, they were so weak. Then he held out a delicate filigree mask for her to wear. "Make sure she doesn't cause any trouble."

"My pleasure." As problems went, she was a very small one. It couldn't be that hard to keep track of one tiny human in a building full of shifters. Not with magic on his side.

"How the hell did he do that?" The mask had come out of nowhere.

"Magic."

"Nevermind, I don't really care. Let's get something straight, you don't get to touch me!"

"I'm touching you just fine," he chuckled.

This man might not be as crazy as his friend, but she

wasn't going to get her hopes up. "I don't suppose you'd let me borrow your phone?"

"I don't have one on me, but I'm sure we can find a charger that will work. We can get you a more appropriate outfit too."

"Since I won't be staying, my wardrobe insufficiency seems moot." Izzy pressed against the solid wall of muscles holding her hostage. *Daaamn!* It was really too bad she couldn't stay plastered to him all night. In another world, she'd be all over him.

"Suite yourself, I guess the closet it is then." He bent and scooped her into his arms like she weighed less than a feather and headed for the damn pantry.

"Stop! You can't just lock me up."

"I have no choice, you heard Aggiron. If you won't join the party, you'll stay here."

"Fine! For heaven's sake put me down, you're covered in static electricity."

"I think I'll keep you right where you are, oddly it works for me." He handed her the mask that dangled from his fingers and changed course, backing out of the swinging doors instead.

She inhaled deeply, preparing to scream. Someone here must be level headed, she needed to get their attention.

"It won't have the effect you're hoping for." The deep rumble vibrated through his chest, the awesome one she was pressed against. She looked up into his decorative mask, two beautiful blue-grey eyes peered out. Wow, she'd never seen anyone like the nordic ice warrior who carried her, at least not in person. His pale ivory skin fit his glossy streaked hair, but it was all wrong for his physique. She hadn't expected a silver fox, not from the solid muscles that carried her like she weighed less than an ounce. Maybe he dyed it?

"How old are you?" *Crap! Rude much lately?*

"Two hundred seven at my last reckoning."

Okay, obviously he was sensitive to age questions. Must be prematurely graying since he couldn't be more than thirty. Behind his gunmetal gray mask, there wasn't a wrinkle on him, nor an ounce of fat. He must live in a gym. Who had time for a cosplaying weight-room diva? *Oh crap!* They'd left the busy party and headed toward the empty rooms.

"Help!"

HER PLEASANT SMELL ENGULFED HIM, LIKE BATHING IN wassail, but less sticky. He was already enjoying this assignment more than he'd expected. She fit perfectly in his arms, too bad she was a frail little human. Though her small size meant it wouldn't use much magic to suitably outfit her. He set her on her feet just outside his thick knotty pine door and yanked her back when she tried to escape. She was his ticket into the group, no way would he let her cause a problem. He shoved her into the room and locked the door.

She skittered across the floor, her dark chestnut locks tangled around her shoulders in crazy waves and her chocolate eyes blazing. She was a perfect accoutrement to the rustic lodge furniture. A little wild. "Don't touch me again!" Fear shot through her leaking out her pores with an acrid stench.

"Stop worrying, you smell awful when you worry."

"I want to call the sheriff, now!" She backed up against the opposite wall, as far from him as she could get. Scanning the room, probably in search of a weapon.

Everyone would be happier if she were more relaxed, including her. Besides, his future depended on it. He turned away from her and shifted his hand scraping off a few scales with his fang as he bit deep enough that blood flooded his tongue. Chewing the mix into a paste, he contemplated the spell. She'd believe assistance was on the way. He spoke softly and spit the mix in his hand. "Let's get you that phone." He stalked to his dresser and covered the back of his phone with the blood and scale mix. He held it out for her and waited patiently while she mustered the courage to take it from him.

A spark zipped through him again when they touched, must be a low humidity day. He shook it off and spoke the words of the spell.

She stared at the phone, blinked a couple times, then looked up at him. The spell had allayed her fear. A twinge of regret shot through him, but he ruthlessly squashed it. This was for the best.

"They'll be here as soon as they can." She spoke quietly, still under his influence.

"What do you say we get you dressed and join the party?"

"Yeah, okay."

She absently handed the phone back to him. They needed her to submit, but this left a nasty taste in his mouth. He much preferred her feisty spirit.

CHAPTER 3

Izzy adjusted her mask. Farryn had found a costume in her size, a beautiful amethyst lace that fit like a glove. The sheriff would be here soon and she'd enjoy the party while she waited. Everything was coming together, so why did she feel something was off? She practiced a smile she didn't feel and headed out of the restroom.

Farryn wore a silver dragon costume that was perfectly tailored to display his trim muscular chest. Her fingers itched to feel it. For an ice warrior, he was one hot cookie. Something about him attracted her more than any man she could remember... ever.

"Would you like some wassail?" He held a mug out to her.

"What is it?" A cinnamon stick rose out of a spicy appley-orange scented drink that warmed her fingers through the mug.

"A mulled cider." His blue-gray eyes sparkled over the rim as he took a drink. He was dangerously good looking. She needed to stop mooning over him and focus on getting her car out of the ditch. A chill ran down her spine, she might be stuck here all night.

She glanced out the window, it was still a solid blizzard outside. She took a small sip savoring the sweet spices, hoping they would warm away her sudden chill. "Is there a hotel in town the sheriff can take me to?"

"If he's able to make it in this weather." A man in a beautiful blue dragon costume standing nearby pointed at the windows. "You can always stay in my room." He winked at her.

"There's plenty of room here. Izzy, this is Becket, he works with Aggiron."

"Charmed indeed." Becket bowed, taking her mug and kissing her knuckles. "Would you like to dance?" He offered his elbow to her and handed her mug to Farryn, who frowned into it.

"I'd love to." Her fingers slid across his smooth scales. His costume was amazing, like a second skin. A flash of heat warmed her, and she squashed thoughts of running her hands along Farryn's costume. Better use this opportunity to borrow Becket's phone and get an update on her car's extraction. She couldn't stay here overnight or she might make another stupid mistake.

FARRYN STRUGGLED TO SWALLOW THE GROWL CLIMBING HIS throat. Definitely two steps backward in introducing himself well to the team. But the scent of orange spice that heated the air when she'd touched Becket infuriated him. Thoughts of her hands on him were even now eating through his brain. Shaking his head, he attempted to dislodge them. This woman would not destroy his ability to charm the team. He had a goal, and he was going to stick to it, so what if her laughter stirred his desire to yank her from Becket's grasp.

"She's a beauty." Admired Barlowe, the head of the dragon

council. He was standing next to him, watching him steam over Becket's usurpation. Fates, this woman was destroying his dreams without even trying.

"Yes, she is." *Dumb, stupid,* what was he saying.

"Will you claim her?" Barlowe turned and watched him like an insect on a mounting pin.

Which reaction would advance his career more? "We've only just met." He kicked himself as the words slid from his treacherous mouth.

"My experience was immediate. I knew my mate was mine." Fates, was he being dismissed as indecisive? He thought the dragon council didn't allow mated dragons. "But of course, *she* was a dragoness."

"Your loss is immeasurable." That explained things, he was no longer mated. He searched his mind for the proper etiquette. All dragonesses passed before the rift, so he'd been without his mate for centuries now. But Farryn could smell his pain, like fresh rain on a high alpine meadow.

"Yet... she still guides my actions." Like most of the unoccupied guests, he was watching Izzy and Becket dance again.

Nonplussed, he could only imagine the pain. His closest experience was the loss of his mother. Which had been more about Farryn's role in killing her and his father living with a damaged soul. Yep... not something he planned on signing up for, especially with a weak human.

FARRYN CRINGED AS KIERAN SWAGGERED UP BESIDE HIM. Another of the recent returnees, his mere presence rubbed Farryn's scales the wrong way.

"Hello Barlowe, sir." He bowed nearly to the floor. *Suckup.* Only a handful of the returnees were strong enough to vie for a seat on the council, unfortunately this was one of them.

"Evening, Kieran."

Farryn's heart sank. How had *he* gotten noticed by the head of the council?

Barlowe cleared his throat. "Farryn, bring your lady friend by my suite in the morning." Then he set off toward Aggiron.

"Yes sir." Farryn's scales were puffed up by ten feet at least. A personal invitation nonetheless. Kieran could drown in scale dust.

"Ha, good luck convincing her." Now didn't that just suck the wind right out of his scales. When he imagined her refusal, his tail twitched. He was tempted to bash Kieran in his smug little face with it, but couldn't figure out how to make it look like an accident.

"Think I'll go introduce myself, pity to let Becket have all the fun." He was heading toward Izzy when Farryn's suppressed growl escaped his icy chest and rumbled low and deadly across the room. He turned back and tsked at him. "If you like it, put a mark on it."

Farryn stood as immovable as an iceberg. He wouldn't let Kieran under his scales, not over a human. Losing his cool in front of the team was not an option. Her laughter slid across his scales. Bless the Fates... don't let it happen.

CHAPTER 4

Izzy saw Farryn stiffen from across the room. Obviously, he didn't like the man he was speaking with. His sexy rumble filtered over her, washing her in endorphins. *So damn sexy.* Every man in the place seemed to be vying for her attention, but he held back. He was confident and determined, two traits she admired. Giving her space made him more attractive.

"Let's dance." The man spun her around, gripping her arm too hard.

"Ouch." Even though she cringed, Kieran didn't lighten his grip.

"Come on, let's give him a good show." She tried to pull away, but he focused his sickeningly flat eyes on her. Animosity washed over her. He clearly didn't want to dance with her, so what was his game? The music slowed, and he pulled her close to his chest. Revulsion mixed with fear as he caught her in a close embrace. His breath tickled her ear. "Your smell is divine, I see why he likes you. Want to make him jealous?"

She turned her head away when he leaned in to kiss her. He just laughed and kissed her neck instead.

"Your distress will work just as well, maybe better." He pressed himself against her, he was disturbingly turned on by her disinterest.

"Let me go!" She pushed against his chest. His tail wrapped around her ankle, pulling her off balance and forcing her to cling to him. Was that animatronics?

"I could break you with only two fingers, I'd suggest you play nice." He hissed at her through clenched teeth. She looked up into his face and blanched at the size of his fangs. Talk about taking a costume too far. He definitely won the asshole-of-the-night award.

A low vibration shook the air next to her, and she was relieved when he swirled them revealing a familiar gunmetal gray dragon costume. Farryn's arm slid comfortingly around her waist and pulled her against his solid chest. Hello sexy, her knight in shining armour. "Enough Kieran."

"Come to claim your mate?" His voice was pitched a little too loud for the intimacy of their stance.

Izzy melted into Farryn's chest, relieved as Kieran's tail finally slid from her ankle. "Catch you later, sweetheart."

Izzy had enjoyed a lovely evening despite the fact that the sheriff never showed. But, the white wall of snow blocking the windows was a great excuse. It wasn't like she was out in the snow freezing. Instead, she was safe and warm inside and had to admit this celebration was entertaining. The bride and groom had been very welcoming when she'd thanked them for letting her crash their wedding. Farryn was a complete gentleman and gorgeous eye candy to boot. And he liked her... like *really* liked her. She was finally catching a break. He didn't appear to have any ulterior motive other than keeping her safe. At first, she thought that was ridiculous, then she'd met that awful Kieran fellow. He was a bad apple.

She shook off the bad vibes and focused on something a little happier. She was looking forward to some snuggle time with Farryn. Despite his obvious attraction, he had been politely hands off all evening. With any luck that would change soon.

"So, where am I going to sleep?" She hoped he'd invite her to his room. Not so they could sleep together, just to snuggle.

"Turns out there's not a single room free, but you'll have mine. I'll sleep on one of the couches in the lounge." His icy eyes sparkled like diamonds in the hall light as they traced her curves. Heat flushed through her veins following their caress.

"Oh, I'll take the couch." She wasn't going to run him out of his own room.

"No, I insist. A door will keep you safe." They were almost to his room, the one she didn't want to be responsible for kicking him out of.

Summoning her courage, she took a deep breath and just asked for what she wanted. "How about we share it, we're both adults?"

THE THOUGHT OF HER ON HIS BED HAD HIM HELPLESSLY HORNY, as if he was an untried hatchling again. Mating hormone spiked his blood supply. His fangs lowered in his mouth as he thought of marking her. *Woah!* He was a life altering misunderstanding away from marking her, definitely had to come clean first. Make her understand that he really was a dragon, not just a man in a fabulous costume. Her orange spice swirled around the hallway. He ushered her into his room to keep it all to himself. Nobody else should smell her. If he came clean now, she might not help him win over Barlowe in the morning.

"I smell sandalwood."

Damn, his hormone levels were high enough that a human could smell them, so much for keeping this from the council. Might as well send all caution to the wind.

"I need a favor."

"Okay, how can I help?"

"I'm competing for a promotion. Tomorrow the man in charge wants to meet you." Well it was something like that at least.

"Sure."

Her breathing was fast and deep, he could smell her interest in him. It was twirling around his own mating scent, permeating the room. He stepped closer to her, his scales lifting in anticipation. She reached her hand out tentatively to touch his scales. A blue arc shot from her fingers, surging through him and quick as a shiver, he was in human form.

"*Mine.*" Rumbled from deep in his soul. She'd switched him to human form with only a touch, the one true sign of a mate. Proof of his blood-borne magic's reaction to her particular genetic makeup. He was in awe. After so many years, he never expected to actually find her.

"Wow, naked. Your body is fine, nothing to be ashamed about here. But that is one kick-ass costume."

CHAPTER 5

Izzy stretched her arms over her head and pushed out her toes. Farryn's arm still rested on her waist, the humming energy between them felt marvelous. After recovering from the initial shock of his naked state, he'd put on pajama pants and offered her one of his shirts. That was one crazy quick change costume. He'd claimed dragons were real, as if she'd believe such a silly notion. She liked his playful side and snuggling with him had brought her the best night's sleep of her life.

She'd always been sensitive, but last night had gotten intense. She could feel Farryn's attraction to her. It was warm and smooth and slid right in, next to her own building desire. A warm fuzziness in her stomach, like puppies and roses. A stark contrast to the stinging scorpion crawl she felt burning from Kieran. She didn't want to run into him again today.

"Good morning." Farryn rolled over and dragged her on top of him. Her legs slid apart straddling his hips, and she pressed against his muscular chest. He ran his fingers into her hair and tilted her face up. Then pulled her into his kiss.

It was warm and demanding. Like he was claiming a right and her body responded in agreement. She parted her lips, inviting him in. He swept his tongue across hers and fire roared up her spine, igniting a desire for him like none before. Planting her hands in the covers on either side of his face, she leaned forward to deepen the kiss.

They parted on a gasp for air as he tugged her hair back and peppered her neck with kisses.

"I want to explore you thoroughly, but we have an appointment this morning." His voice was gravely from the force of his desire.

An icky twinge raced through her mind, as if she could feel his reluctance. Was he just using her? "Well, let's get going." No point putting off the inevitable. She had very high standards and few ever lived up to them.

A HEADACHE CREEPED UP ON IZZY, GETTING SHARPER THE closer she got to Barlowe's suite. By the time the door opened, a queasiness had settled in her stomach. She wasn't surprised to find Kieran already inside all decked out in his oily black costume again.

"Awe, the love birds have arrived." They followed Kieran into the living room. A fire crackled in the large stone fireplace warming the dark leather sofa she sank into.

"Still haven't marked her?" Kieran's animosity spiked her head ache.

"Leave it alone." A deep rumble rode across the room and shook her senses. A beautifully majestic black dragon entered the room. Her head throbbed, she'd give almost anything for some ibuprofen and an ice pack. "Izzy, I'd like you to meet Barlowe. He's the head of the dragon council."

"Nice to meet you."

"The pleasure is all mine." He bowed to her, then took a seat next to Kieran. "It isn't often that I meet a possible mate. You have proven very hard to find."

She wasn't surprised that they had a hard time finding people to join their cosplay group. Not everyone would find it a fun way to spend their time. Last night had been fun, she wouldn't mind joining them again. Thankfully none of the women had worn the elaborate dragon costumes, they must be hot.

He turned, addressing Farryn. "By order of the council, mated dragons must be bound. When do you plan to mate?"

Participating in their role play with her head aching so much was challenging. "Quick question, why do they have to be bound?"

"Dragons are too volatile after they mate. Mating hormones take over, destroying logic and common sense. We would never remain hidden from humans if mated dragons kept their powers." Boy, they had really elaborate rituals. She didn't want to ruin it for everyone, but she wasn't sure she wanted to join a group that took things so seriously. Would she get kicked out if she messed up? Talk about ruining your weekend.

Unfortunately, Kieran had sat down next to her. When she gripped her head again, he ran his fingers down her arm. It took all her control not to cringe.

"I wonder if this is a side effect of the spell?"

"Spell?" *Crap*, she already regretted engaging him.

"The one with the sheriff. He did tell you didn't he?" There was a glee to his darkness that made Izzy's skin crawl as it washed over her.

Maybe that was why she felt so hot and sick. She looked at Farryn "Did you give me something?"

"No." He was looking at her with a puppy-caught-piddling sort of look.

"What did you do? Tell me everything, right now." An awful wave of regret washed over her, it made her stomach curl. But it wasn't her regret... it was his. What was happening to her?

"I helped you think you'd called the sheriff."

"So, the sheriff was never called?" She looked around the group of men, all decked out in their cosplay finest. Had they tricked her for the sake of a game?

"No." Her stomach sank, he'd lied to her. She knew better, but she'd trusted him anyway. Rising from the couch, desperate to escape the sudden assault of regrets, she tried to block them. Distinguishing between Farryn, Kieran, and herself became impossible. Negative energy was sweeping over her from each of them. No point wasting another minute of her time. There was nothing here for her now. She'd be safer out in the storm.

CHAPTER 6

Barlowe called after him, "Give her space, Farryn!" But Farryn moved to follow Izzy out of the suite, anyway. The guards at the door grabbed him and pulled him back into the room.

"Let her have some time. With this weather, she won't go anywhere." Barlowe motioned for one of his guards to follow her. "They'll keep track of her."

Farryn turned on Kieran, fury burning through him. Somehow, the creep had set him up. "You did this on purpose."

"Don't blame me, I only asked if her headache was from your spell?"

"She doesn't understand about dragons. Probably thinks I poisoned her." Grief and anger mixed in him. He wanted to blame Kieran, but this was all his fault. Using magic on her without a thought to the consequences had been a stupid move.

Becket and Aggiron entered followed by two other members of the team. "Farryn!" Becket shook his hand. "This is Dyson, and that's Eloi. Camden should be here any minute."

"Hey." He should be thrilled, this had been his goal all along. Without Izzy, it just felt cold. His problems with Izzy would have to wait, he needed to focus on the here and now, keep it together.

"I hear you've got a binding in your future. Congratulations." Eloi shook his hand.

"I wouldn't count on that." Kieran jumped out of the way as Farryn's tail whipped the couch.

"No?" A wicked spark shot through Becket's eyes. "Does that mean she's available? She's hot, I'm game."

Farryn slammed the door to his room, he couldn't help himself. He was so furious. That sniveling little fool had probably blown his chances of getting on the council. Kieran was going to pay.

Smoke swirled from his nostrils filling the room with his inky irritation. If it was the last thing he did, he'd make sure that idiot never made it on the team.

First order of business was to dig up as much information on Kieran as possible. With as shady as that dragon acted, there was bound to be a scandal somewhere. He plopped himself in front of the desk and pulled up his tablet. Time to find out what he'd been up to the last hundred years or so.

As he brought up his search program, he thought about the second order of business. This mate situation needed to be settled once and for all. He wasn't going to give up his powers for a human, that would be crazy. Should have let her call the stupid sheriff yesterday, then none of this would have happened. Well that had a very easy solution. Call the damn sheriff himself and get her bundled up and on her way.

He pulled out his phone and looked up the Dragondell Sheriff's number.

"Hello, I'd like to report an accident."

IZZY'S FINGERS WERE FREEZING. SHE SHOULDN'T HAVE LEFT IN a huff. At least, not without calling the sheriff. The hike out to her car hadn't been that bad, but digging out the door and tailpipe had completely soaked her gloves. No matter how much she dug, there was no way she could get out of the ditch without a tow truck. Snow started falling again, blanketing the car windows. She would warm up, then walk along the road. It couldn't be more than a few miles to the next building. There was at least an hour or two before sunset. As long as she hurried she'd be fine.

Slamming her hand on the steering wheel, she cursed her stupid choices. When would she stop being so gullible? Just because he was sexy and polite didn't mean he was trustworthy. If she'd spent more time working on her car problem instead of mooning over a hot guy, she wouldn't be freezing now. She blasted the furnace and laid her gloves over the vents. Hopefully they would dry enough to be useful. She'd give them ten minutes, then she was heading out.

On the street above, a horn honked followed by a loud crunch. She threw open her door to wave down the car when a tumble of snow brought a skidding slide of bloody deer down the edge of the ditch. God, the size of those antlers, please don't let her be impaled. She braced for the impact, but the force of it knocked her chest into a locked down vice. If she ever took another breath, it'd be a miracle.

CHAPTER 7

A loud thump at the door brought Farryn out of his rabbit hole search. He'd been able to piece together a rudimentary timeline for Kieran over the last fifty years. It wasn't much, but it was a start. As he stretched, another round of loud thumping started on his door. *This better be good.*

"Just a second." He grumbled and yanked open the door.

Barlowe stood arms crossed, scowling at him. "I had an interesting talk with the local sheriff. Turns out that accident you called in had signs of a tousle and blood all over it. Care to explain?"

Fear slid in and got comfortable under his scales. She hadn't looked injured when she arrived yesterday. "Did you ask Izzy about it?"

"She's not with you?"

"No." He'd felt relief when she wasn't in his room earlier, now he kicked himself for not searching her down. "I called the sheriff to come pick her up."

Barlowe leaned out the door and questioned his guard.

"He says he followed her here and left when she didn't come out."

His scales shifted as fear started to claw into his soft underside. "Where is she?"

"She's your mate, you ought to know."

"I never claimed her." He could no longer keep his scales from twitching.

"Denying the Fates is never a good idea. I get your reluctance to claim a human, but they are the reason we came to this world."

"I have goals. She interferes with them." All the lives sacrificed in order to form the rift that brought them here was overwhelming. But he hadn't asked for the rift.

Barlowe widened his nostrils and breathed in slow and steady. He put his hand on Farryn's shoulder to stop his fidgeting. "I'm smelling fear, not disappointment."

THE SUN WAS BEGINNING TO SET BEHIND THE MOUNTAINS, HE only had a half hour at most before the temperature started to drop dangerously low for a human. Farryn rushed toward the ditch. A sheriff's jeep was parked to the side of the road, getting buried in fresh falling snow. He needed to find her. In his anger he'd planned to send her away, but he realised now he could never do that.

Icy claws gripped his chest as he saw the blood and broken glass around her car. Something had been severely hurt. Panic filled him. He fought to suppress it. Searching for her spicy orange scent, he breathed deep. Over the deer's blood he caught a faint trace. She'd been here, not long ago. He shot out in the direction of her scent.

"Hey, where are you going?" The sheriff called, but someone else would have to deal with him. Farryn had a mate to find. By the intensity of her scent, he knew she was injured.

Tracking her across the disturbed snow, he wondered why she was chasing after an injured buck. Walking into a field, injured, in the middle of a blizzard. Not a wise decision. She had some explaining to do. Just as soon as he had her healed and bundled up in his bed.

He found he could live without a lot of things in life; a mother, a father who loved him, his blessed seat on the council. What he'd recently discovered and hated to admit was, he couldn't bear to live without one feisty little human.

AS HE CLAWED HIS WAY OVER A CRAG, FARRYN CAUGHT SIGHT of Izzy slumped over a fallen log. Praise the Fates, don't let him be too late. He rushed over to her side, careful not to disturb her while he searched for her injuries.

"Hey little human, why are you so far out in the woods?" He gently lifted her hair back from her face. Her lips were tinged with blue.

"My knight in a shining... dragon costume."

He bent down beside her and cleared an area for her to lay out flat.

"Deer's hurt. Got lost following it. Can't catch... breath." She was panting quick and shallow. Her elbows pulled tight against her sides and she clutched at her chest.

"I'm going to heal you. Okay?" She'd finally understand this wasn't a live action role play adventure. He dug his claws in deep until blood dripped down his arms then stripped the scales in a groove down to his elbows. He crushed them in his claws blending his blood in, infusing the mix with his magic. When he had enough to coat her chest, he hooked his claw on her zipper and pulled her jacket open.

"I need you to lay flat on your back." She shifted to the area he'd cleared and looked up into his eyes. She was trusting him. He wouldn't let her down again. Spreading her jacket apart, he slit her shirt right down the middle. Shifting to human form, he worked the mix across her chest and rib while quietly starting the incantation. This healing magic was stronger than he usually performed, so he let his blood continue to flow onto the mix as he chanted.

Her eyes were closed peacefully, and the color was starting to return to her lips. He'd nearly finished when claws dug deep between his shoulder blades shooting burning pain down his back and arms. Despite the risk, he rolled to the side Kieran's claws ripping through his skin.

"I thought I'd get to kill your mate. Didn't realise you were out here too."

Izzy ducked behind a fallen log, clutching her jacket together. Farryn moved between them, he couldn't let Kieran near her. Releasing his fire, he hit Kieran full force in the chest toppling him backwards. It wouldn't be enough. The healing spell had sapped his strength.

"Get away from her." His strength was dropping too fast. He was losing too much blood between the wounds on his back and the ones still dripping from his arms. Kieran laughed a deep disturbing roar.

"This will be the perfect end to you. Freezing with your pathetic mate." He stepped around Farryn, pulled Izzy to her feet, and ripped the jacket from Izzy's back. She'd never last long at this temperature. She had to survive, he needed her. Fates, he loved her more than life. He struggled to get to her as the world faded to black.

CHAPTER 8

Pulling the tatters of her clothes around her the best that she could, Izzy sank next to Farryn. He was covered in blood, crystals of it forming around him in the snow. The sun was setting, they didn't have much time left. He'd healed her, just to die in her stead. She screamed in frustration. They were only in this mess because of her, since her heart had been hurt. Just because she'd cared too much too quickly. She hadn't given him a chance to explain, to show her he really was a dragon.

God. He was a *dragon.* She was in a fairy tale, but it had turned dark and deadly in the blink of an eye.

"Tell me what to do to help you." She pressed her jacket remnants against his bleeding arms, trying to staunch the blood flow. He needed to wake up. If she could roll him over, maybe she'd be able to bind the worst of his wounds. She struggled to drag him to his side and his eyes fluttered open.

"What do I do?" She begged him for help.

"Leave me." His voice crackled with pain.

She shook her head, tears freezing on her lashes. "No. Never." Nothing in life was important without him.

He groaned as she flopped him on his belly. The skin of his upper back was in ribbons. She stripped off the remains of her shirt and pressed them into his shoulders.

"You have to do that healing thing again." She was shouting at him, but couldn't help it. Death wasn't allowed. He was her *dragon*!

"My mother died in childbirth, please don't make me the reason my mate dies too. I'd never survive that." How could he be asking her to leave him?

"You'll die if I leave you here."

"No, I'm a dragon. I can heal. You however, will freeze if you don't get to shelter."

"Well I'm not leaving you. So you better start your healing soon." He'd improved since she'd packed his wounds in ice and stopped the bleeding. Surrounded by so much snow, it was a miracle that he wasn't frozen solid. She was shivering so badly her teeth were at risk of cracking.

"Come here." He had a surprising amount of command in his voice for someone so close to death. She leaned in towards him and he yanked her against his chest, wrapping her in his warmth.

"If you refuse to leave, you give me no choice but to mate you. My fire is the only way you'll survive."

She snuggled in closer, loving his smooth sandalwood scent. "If we're going to die, I might as well humor you."

His hands slid up her ribs cupping her breasts through her bra. She was feeling warmer already. Her legs rested next to his hips as she straddled him. Leaning forward, she brushed her lips gently over his.

He growled and cupped her head pulling her in for a deep

kiss, tongue spearing into her mouth. Her entire body was no longer cold. A smoldering fire sparked deep in her senses.

Rapping his hands in her hair, he pulled her face back. Gazing deep in her eyes, like he could read her soul he whispered to her. "Mating is for life. You'll be *Mine* forever."

"Will I turn into a dragon? Like a werewolf?" He chuckled and his eyes softened.

"No, dragonhood is not contagious. You will however take on part of my DNA. That's the only way to keep you warm. I've lost too much blood to get you back to shelter."

"Why not use your magic again?" He tilted her head back and licked along her jugular. Warmth spread deep within her and she ground against his erection. That part seemed to be working just fine despite his injuries.

"My blood and scales are my magic. I've lost too much to cast big spells, but I can still make the protein to allow you to accept my blood." With a flick of his wrist, her remaining clothes melted away. He tilted his hips rubbing along her core. She was slick with desire.

"Is it just sex?" She wanted him deep inside her.

"No. It's a blood exchange, it could never be just sex with you. I love you too much."

Her heart skipped a beat. He loved her. Happiness shot through her system despite their dire situation. She'd finally found the one. Totally sucked that it was right before she froze to death.

"Wait, blood exchange, like a transfusion?" How would they do that out here?

"Sort of, I'll bite you here," he lightly pressed his fangs on her delicate shoulder. "And then my body will make the proteins necessary to fight your antibody response."

"How do I get the proteins?"

"You'll have to take in my blood." That sounded totally disgusting.

"Ick, like drink it?"

"Yes, you have to get enough of the proteins or my blood will kill you. Do you accept me?"

"Yes." She whispered breathlessly. He owned her heart, might as well give him her body too.

He slid into her thick folds. Arching his back to go deeper into her core. He started a slow pumping that built to a furious demand. Skin slapping against skin. She kissed him, twirling tongues together bringing her to the edge of release.

He twisted her hair around his hand and that's when he struck. His fangs going fast and deep. She flew over the crest and shuddered with her release as he drank, long pulls draining her blood into his system. She felt his release shoot hot and deep into her core.

As she came down, she thought she should probably be more freaked out than she felt. For heaven's sake she'd just mated a dragon. Too bad she was going to freeze soon. She could already feel the heat draining from her with each drop of blood.

Just as her eyes were getting too heavy to keep open, he ripped his wrist open and forced it against her mouth. The thick tangy blood slid across her tongue and she had to swallow or choke. Desperately, she fought to get away, but he just growled and held her tighter. She was no match for his strength even in his weakened state.

"Drink it." He commanded, blood dripping from his fangs. "You'll die if you don't."

GREY LIGHT OF DAWN SPREAD ACROSS THE SKY SPARKLING FROM the crystals in the newly fallen snow. They'd survived. She snuggled closer to Farryn pulling the blanket around her. Wait.

"How did you get a blanket out here?" He tucked his arm around her the weight a comfortable presence across her waist.

"Magic." He rooted his nose into her hair breathing deep. "I love your scent, spicy orange, just like my favorite wassail."

"We made it." Relief was heavy in her limbs. A peaceful contentment slid across her senses. It felt warm and creamy like Farryn's sandalwood scent. "I think I can sense what you're feeling, like an Empath."

"Really?" He lifted his head and slowly pulled down the blanket. Her nipples peaked in the cold air. "What am I feeling now?" A warm rush of desire spiked her system.

"That's too easy." She rolled over gently brushing his lips with hers, then ran her fingers along his smooth taut muscles and dug in when she felt him twitch.

"Knock it off?" He cringed away from her.

"Ticklish?" She giggled.

"Not hardly, I'm a dragon. We aren't ticklish." He rolled over on top of her, pinning her arms to the ground.

A throat cleared behind him and she tried to disappear under the covers. "I could have used you last night when Kieran attacked." Farryn said.

"We're glad to find you safe." Aggiron entered the clearing and motioned for the others to surround them. "We'd thought you lost when we found Kieran covered in your blood."

"Thankfully my mate is quick thinking." He bent and kissed her forehead.

Becket entered the clearing carrying a large bag, then upended it on the blanket. "Thought you could use a few supplies." Clothes and boots tumbled in a heap and Izzy grabbed her clothes, pulling them under the covers to dress.

"I am in your debt." Farryn addressed the team and bowed to the two in front of him.

"We'll discuss how you'll repay us later. For now, let's celebrate your mating. There's time enough tomorrow to plan your binding.

As she climbed out from under the covers, Becket was there with a helping hand to steady her.

"Oh darling, blue is so much better than silver. Now you'll always wonder." He winked at her. Farryn's tail whipped out almost faster than her eyes could track, sending him across the clearing. Becket laughed as he pulled himself off the tree he'd been shoved into.

"I can't wait to meet your mate." Becket blanched, the rest of the team joined Farryn in a boisterous fit of laughter.

SUPPORTING HER IN HIS ARMS, FARRYN BREATHED DEEPLY. HE was nervous to lose his powers, but any sacrifice was worth the life of his mate. The fever that came with mating had done its job and kept her warm through the cold. Would he continue to keep her safe?

Anger spread through him when he saw Kieran. Arms restrained, guards were leading him toward Barlowe's private transport. Without a thought of the consequences, Farryn whipped his tail out, stabbing the tip through his throat. Blood burst from his mouth as he collapsed onto the ground. Half the guards rushed him into the transport, while the other half surrounded Farryn and Izzy.

Barlowe waved them off. "This is precisely the kind of issue we want to avoid. Imagine if there were humans around. You will report for your binding on Monday." Without waiting for a reply, he climbed into the transport.

"We'll take care of him. He won't hurt another dragon." Aggiron followed after the group.

Becket walked past Farryn and stopped next to Izzy.

Bowing, he took her hand and kissed her knuckles. "I look forward to seeing you again." He dodged just in time as Farryn's tail whipped over his head. A deep, menacing growl shook the air.

Izzy started to giggle, then it broke into a full out laugh. "I'm sorry, this is a totally unreasonable response."

"You're *Mine*, nobody gets to touch you." Little curls of smoke twirled from his nostrils. Monday might not come soon enough.

"Silly dragon," Izzy pulled him into her arms. "You're *Mine*."

EPILOGUE

Farryn's muscles tightened, pulling his scales toward the surface of his skin. Stomping back along the railing, he settled between Izzy and the street, desperate to block her from yet another car full of simpering humans. His feisty little mate wrapped her arms around her knees, pulling her legs closer to her chest, as if she could disappear into the chair. Where the hell was the realtor? With people traipsing along the sidewalk and filing into the mortuary, he was powerless to help her. He couldn't perform a spell out in the open with an audience. Humans didn't know about dragons, and that was how the council wanted it to remain. A dragon realtor wouldn't have shown a home next to a mortuary to an Empath. A situation like this was exactly what he'd wanted to avoid, but she'd insisted on supporting her friend. Through her ignorance, the uninitiated human had rendered him incapable of comforting his mate.

"I thought this lady was your friend." The shadow along her brow darkened, and he regretted adding to her discomfort.

"I should have given her a better list of requirements. Something like this never crossed my mind."

Her human friend had another five minutes, then they were leaving. He couldn't keep an unshielded Empath next to a wake for Fate's sake.

A car pulled into the driveway, and relief flooded through him.

"About time." They hadn't even started the search, but he was ready to call it a day.

"Give it a rest." Izzy's features relaxed as she rushed past him to greet her friend.

As soon as they got inside, he'd slip into the garage and cast a blocking spell while Izzy started the tour.

"It's so good to see you." The woman's shrill voice stabbed at his eardrums. Biting back the nasty comment riding his tongue, Farryn forced his lips into a smile. Today would test his restraint.

"Farryn, I'd like you to meet Winnie." The two friends strolled up the walkway side-by-side, arms locked together, as if the other might vanish upon letting go.

"I've heard so much about you." He shook her outstretched hand, trying to extinguish his irritation before Izzy felt it rumbling below the surface. Stepping back, he made room for the women to enter the house. With any luck, his spell would save the day and allow this listing to better tailor their search.

IZZY FORCED HER GAZE FROM THE CORDED MUSCLES RIPPLING along Farryn's shoulders as they pulled up to the second house. She squeezed her arms across her over sensitive breasts, intent on ignoring the heat building in her core. His dampening spell had worked a little too well, removing all the background chatter she'd used to dam up the burning desire from mating heat. Now it crashed through her in violent waves.

"Perhaps we should reschedule." Farryn rubbed his hands along his face, burying his fingers in his hair. "Although, this listing has more potential than the last."

Grasping onto the distraction, Izzy shifted her attention to the latest house. Thick columns and a deep porch invited her to explore inside the cozy bungalow. She liked it already. Hopping out, she escaped the hormone laden Jeep and met Winnie on the steps.

"This is beautiful."

"I thought you'd appreciate its charm."

"You were right." A warm wave of interest washed over her as Farryn joined them on the porch. Dang, even this much charm couldn't distract her for long.

Winnie's purse started buzzing, and she handed the key to Farryn before digging for her phone. "That must be the listing agent. You two head in, I'll join you in a sec."

Biting her lower lip, Izzy crushed her desire down, and followed Farryn. Thankfully, the charm continued inside with moldings, casings, paneling, and built-ins. She was in heaven. Everywhere she looked, detailed finishes shined.

"What's the list price on this?" Farryn brushed his fingertips up her spine.

Goosebumps sprinted across her skin, and her breath caught. Pulling away from his touch, she stepped into the kitchen. "You can't touch me."

Farryn trailed after her, his breath hot against her nape. "I can't not touch you." His voice, rough with desire, pulled at her resolve and she turned to look up at his face. Heat sparked through his gaze and he yanked her against him.

Breasts pressed against his solid chest, warmth spread through her, raising her nipples into hard taut pebbles. His nostrils flared, and he slid his hands down her sides, pulling her against his rock hard erection. Step by step, he backed her toward the edge of the counter.

"Should we take the kitchen on a test spin?"

Farryn hoisted her onto the counter and slid his rough hands up her thighs, spreading her legs to lean between them. When his thumb brushed against her panties, she moaned softly, thankful she'd worn a skirt despite the chilly weather. Farryn slid his arms under her legs, pulling her to the edge. Seated so close to the sink, she tipped to the side, and he grasped the faucet to keep her from falling in. She wrapped her arms around him and pulled him into a kiss, desperate to taste his lips. Brushing her hand along his solid length, she pinched the tip as she nipped on his lower lip. He twitched, a crack reverberated through the room, and an icy shower shocked her system, pulling her out of her heated daze.

Farryn held a broken faucet handle in his grip. Water sprayed out in an uncontrolled fountain, flooding the counter before dripping onto the floor. Farryn yanked her out of the way, dropping her feet to the floor as rivulets of water rushed from her soaked clothes.

"Oh my, what happened?" Winnie rushed into the kitchen. With a human right next to him, Farryn couldn't magic his way out of this. Izzy's mind raced for a way to get her out of here.

"Did you see towels in the laundry room?"

"Yes, I think so." Winnie rushed off to look for them while Farryn ducked under the counter to turn the water valve off. He sat back and plopped into a puddle that was spreading out across the planks of the wooden floor into the breakfast nook.

"Feisty little vixen. This is all your fault." Water dripped from the ends of his hair in great big soaking drops.

She clasped her hand over her mouth, but a giggle escaped her... then another. When she bent over in a fit of laughter, a you're-going-to-pay-for-this smirk tipped his lips upward. He'd make her suffer for laughing like this.

Winnie raced back with a tower of towels and a glower tormenting her face.

"I cannot see the humor in this."

Farryn arched one silver brow at Izzy, but she descended into another fit of laughter, unable to respond.

"I'll have this fixed in a matter of minutes." Farryn assured Winnie as he lifted the top towel off the pile and mopped up the mess.

With an irritated huff, she tossed the remaining towels at Izzy and stomped off toward the front door. "I'll contact the homeowner."

As soon as the front door snicked shut behind her, Izzy rounded on him. "This wasn't my fault."

"You've abused my manhood. Kiss it and make it better." Desire crashed back into her with the image of kissing his stiff length and she had to bite back her moan. Damn dragon.

Scraping the second furrow down his scales in as many hours, Farryn crushed the scales and mixed a few drops of blood together. He smeared the mix on the end of the faucet and started the lyrical chanting. Izzy headed out to ensure that Winnie remained occupied. No need to compound the issues today by exposing a human.

FROM THE MOMENT THEY TURNED INTO THE DRIVE, FARRYN knew this log cabin was brimming with possibilities. Located high above the valley floor, it would have a wonderful view of Dragondell. He hoped the allure carried through to the deck.

"This might be the one." He nudged Izzy's shoulder with his own. Her warm smile ensured she was at least considering it. From the beginning, this cabin had been on the bottom of her list. As a confirmed city girl, being so far out in the backwoods worried her.

A brisk wind rustled through the aspen trees and he breathed deep, filling his lungs with the crisp mountain breeze. The spice of pine and sap swirled around his tongue.

"Let's check around the outside first." Walking along the shoveled path at the side of the house, he pulled open the gate and stepped onto the desk. He'd been looking forward to the view all day. As he rounded the corner, the sulfur stench of burnt eggs smacked him full in the face. His sensitive sinuses burned, and tears leaked from his eyes. He pulled the neck of his shirt over his face.

"Watch out."

"Oh Fates, did you get sprayed?" He turned back, searching for the skunk just in time to catch Izzy. Burying her nose in her scarf, she'd missed the step. He steadied her before responding.

"No, but something did. The spray is all over this desk." Yet again, he would suffer because of his headstrong mate. If their realtor wasn't human, he'd remove this stench. Instead, misery. He glared at her. The sheepish tilt of her head was the only acknowledgement that he had been right.

Izzy scurried around Farryn, rushing toward the railing of the deck. The combination of skunk spray and Farryn's inky wave of darkness clenched her stomach and nausea climbed up her already burning throat. Thankfully, the breeze picked up, and she gasped in a few desperate gulps of clean, crisp mountain air. Her eyes stung and were so blurry she couldn't make out the view. With any luck, Winnie would appreciate the commission she earned from them, since she would never hear the end of this.

"We should go." This day had been one of the biggest disasters she could remember. Why did everything have to be so hard? If her stupid Empath powers weren't overwhelming her, then her domineering dragon was. She'd only agreed to add this location to the list to shut Farryn up and look at how well that worked out. This location was so not worth it.

"Oh no. You will not walk away now. This was the only property on the list that I was interested in and we will check it out." He yanked the glass doors open with a determined grunt.

Unfortunately, the foul smell followed them inside. She wiped her eyes and blinked, trying to clear the blur. The layout was cozy. She liked the high ceiling and rock fireplace. It was grand, but not too big.

"Let's start upstairs, maybe it doesn't stink as much." Winnie started up the stairs, and Izzy followed on her heels, hoping she was correct. They walked through the guest bedrooms and bathrooms.

"Guests would feel comfortable."

Farryn must be thinking of his dragon friends, because these rooms were huge. Plenty of room for humans, and the designer had carried the rustic cabin charm through accents like the hand-hewn log bed.

"I hate to admit it, but they are nice."

"Is the furniture included?"

Winnie scrolled through the listing on her phone. "Fully furnished is optional. We'd have to negotiate a fair price."

She liked this house more and more. But with how their luck was running, the main floor master would feel like a shoebox, or be missing a bathroom, or something. She took a deep breath, then followed Winnie and Farryn down the stairs. Time to find the drawback. At the base of the stairs, they each headed towards a separate door. Jackpot! She'd found the master. It was perfect, just the right size. The sulfur stench was so strong in here, her eyes were watering again. Not able to stand the burn any longer, she rushed to the bathroom door, hoping to rinse her face in the sink. She flung it open and jumped. A scream ripped up her throat. There was a man... A naked man covered in blood, being mauled by a wolf.

Farryn rushed up behind her and pulled her out of the way. The man slipped and fell, clattering among a pile of cans. What in the world? As one skittered across the floor she realized it was a pile of tomato sauce cans.

Shielded by Farryn's enormous back, she was being walked out of the room backwards.

STUPID SKUNKS, IDIOT HUMANS, THEY WERE ALL CONSPIRING against him. She would never be willing to accept this as her home. Not after being assaulted by a tomato wearing jackass. Farryn pulled the door shut and leaned his forehead against it. He had to salvage this.

"I've got a plan. You two stay out of that room." He stomped into the kitchen. The ingredients had to be in here, no one would live in skunk territory without it. He found the peroxide under the sink and baking soda in the fridge. He dumped pine cones out of a glass bowl and squirted a small glop of soap into the bottom, then tossed in a handful of the baking soda, and carried the bowl with the bottle of peroxide back to the bedroom.

"You better give me a great price on that furniture, call it payment for my pain and suffering. For Fate's sake, she saw your penis." The man cowered in the shower, a towel stewed in tomato sauce wrapped around his waist.

"Dude, you're the ones that walked in on me."

Farryn glared at him. People should arm themselves with a little knowledge of the wildlife they would encounter before moving into the backwoods. He dumped the bottle of peroxide into the bowl and handed the mixture to the man.

"Work this into his fur, scrubbing quickly and rinse well. It could bleach his coat a bit, but it'll kill the stench."

"Thanks, I think."

"Like I said, you owe me." He pulled the door closed and stomped back out to the living room. Izzy and Winnie were laughing their silly heads off. As soon as one stopped they'd look at the other and burst back into peels of laughter. The day was shot. He gave up.

"Time to go." He linked his fingers with Izzy's and pulled her toward the front door.

"Thanks Winnie, I'll call you tomorrow." If the skunk smell hadn't assaulted his snout, he'd have smelt the man a mile away. Instead, his mate got flashed. Irritation ripped through him. He should have taken more precautions. Things could have been so much worse. What if that had been someone from the Magic Black Market?

"I'm sorry. I know you were looking forward to seeing this house." She was wiping tears from her eyes and Farryn couldn't tell if it was from the stupid skunk spray or her laughing fit.

He rolled his eyes. "Just get in the Jeep."

"If it makes you feel any better, you were right."

"Of course I was right. We would have avoided this entire travesty of a day if we'd used a dragon realtor."

"Not about that silly, about the cabin."

"Really?" Joy spread through him. He hadn't expected her to like it.

"Yeah, I love it." She slid her arms around his neck, pulling him in for a deep kiss. "Almost as much as you."

He dragged her body closer to his, molding her soft curves to his hard edges, and deepened their kiss. When she came up for air, he snuggled into her neck and whispered in her ear.

"Welcome home, feisty little vixen."

If you loved *Dragon's Masquerade*, please take a moment to leave a review on your favorite bookstore, BookBub, or Goodreads.

Then continue Izzy and Farryn's story in *Dragon's Feast* or meet a brand new couple in *Dragon's Second Chance*.

SKUNK ODOR NEUTRALIZER

Mix together:

- 1 quart of 3% hydrogen peroxide
- 1/4 cup baking soda
- 1 teaspoon liquid dishwashing soap

Warning: This mixture is volatile and likely to explode if stored in a bottle. Mix when you need it and rinse the remainder down the drain. Do not store.

Rub the mixture deep into your furry little angel's coat and scrub until the odor is neutralized. The peroxide will slightly bleach their coat, so don't leave it on for longer than necessary. Rinse thoroughly and enjoy breathing easier.

SNEAK PEAK OF DRAGON'S FEAST

When she saw the caller id, Izzy's stomach dropped. She'd been avoiding her mother for weeks, but couldn't put off her phone calls any longer unless she wanted Theresia to track her down in person. That was the last thing she needed. Since mating her dragon, she'd developed an inability to keep other's emotions from taking her over. It was exacting a huge toll on her life. Farryn, her dragon mate, had to rescue her from the grocery store when a group of Dragondell High School students had an early release day. With any luck, the effects wouldn't be as bad over the phone. She grabbed her coat and prepared for battle, might as well walk down to the community board to get the mail while she talked. Maybe the exercise would keep her calm. On the last ring before the voicemail picked up, Izzy answered.

"Hi, Mom."

"Oh, I didn't expect you to answer. Seems I'm always missing you." Izzy felt the reprimand behind the tone and let it run off her shoulder. It would get worse before it got better, she was sure of it.

"I'm glad I was available." That wasn't a complete lie. The

crisp air bit at her fingers, so she dug in her pockets for her gloves.

"Me too, you sure are busy since you quit your *job* and moved in with that man. Does that little mountain town have any opportunities?"

Oh brother, a hit at Farryn and Dragondell in one sniping complaint. Izzy hunched her shoulders, releasing tension from her neck, and drawing the clean mountain air deep into her lungs. "Nope, no job yet. Just busy unpacking and settling in." She couldn't imagine working in her current condition.

"Well, I can't wait to see your new place."

Oh no, she needed to nix that idea in the bud. There was no way Izzy could handle her mother's volatile emotions in person. Besides, what if she discovered the truth about Farryn? No, she couldn't let her human mother run around a town full of dragons, who knew what damage that might cause? Her pulse picked up, but it wasn't exertion from the incline. She hurried her pace, as if she could outrun this disaster. "I need to focus on the job interviews, and Farryn's very busy at work, his project is almost complete. I'm sure we couldn't be ready for company until the new year." With any luck, she'd find some control before then.

"Speaking of holidays, I was talking with Susy about Thanksgiving. She and Flint said they hadn't heard from you either. We thought it would be fun to have a big friends and family dinner." Nothing seemed farther from fun than cramming herself into her mother's small apartment with all of her cousins' and friends' heightened emotions bombarding her. Besides, how awkward would it be for Farryn. He hadn't even met her family yet; her mother had been traumatizing enough when she helped pack up for the move.

"That won't work."

"We all miss you, and it's not like you moved to another state."

"I know, I'm just trying to settle in." This mating was proving harder than she'd ever expected, and Farryn was pressuring her to have a handfasting, some kind of dragon marriage ceremony. She glanced at the community board for announcements, then headed to their box. Sitting right on top was a thick, heavyweight envelope.

"Save settling in for non-holidays."

Izzy pulled out the envelope and fingered the delicate gold lettering on the front. She'd never received anything so fancy before. It was from the dragon council, and it would thrill Farryn. Stacking it atop the rest of the pile, she started back up the hill to their cabin.

"Life doesn't always fall together as nicely as we want." They had moved in just last week, it seemed a little early to receive something official looking to the house. She shifted through the other mail as she walked.

"Is there some reason you're avoiding us, that man isn't mistreating you, is he?" Avoiding them was critical. The struggle to control her new empathic abilities was only getting worse. Besides, humans weren't aware of dragons and they wanted to keep it that way.

With a sigh, she bundled the mail together. There were plenty of things addressed to her, but it was all junk.

"Of course not, Farryn is the best part of my new life." She pushed the door open and set the pile of mail on top of the credenza. Her fingers trailed along it as she started into the house again.

Well, that was the excitement for the day. She could start getting dinner ready, or maybe read a book, but nobody needed her. Not for a single thing. Even though she hadn't liked her previous job, at least she'd felt useful, like her life had purpose. Right now, she felt very low indeed. She loved Farryn, since the second he'd swept her up into his arms, but mating a dragon was harder than it seemed.

"Well I'm worried about you. It's not like you to avoid your friends." Her mom was right, and the isolation made it more painful. Izzy looked around the empty cabin. She needed a dragon survival pack: burn gel, gauze bandages, styptic powder, just to name a few, and that didn't even cover the emotional cost. Leaving behind her crappy apartment for the beautiful cabin in the woods wasn't bad, nor did she think twice about quitting her job. But she didn't realize how isolated she would be. It had never crossed her mind that she wouldn't be able to visit her friends, or even make any new ones. Every time she was around another person, their emotions attacked her. She needed to find someone who could help.

Besides, how could normal humans be around dragons? Without the healing cells mates received when they paired off with a dragon, there would be an awful mishap. Just last week Farryn had sneezed and roasted her favorite plant, imagine if that had been Susy or Flint. Not an acceptable risk at all.

Maybe magic could protect them. It couldn't be that hard to create some kind of talisman. *That was it!* She would get Farryn to create one for her, one that blocked her powers. Then she could see her friends. Sitting in the woods while the world happened outside the door wasn't for her. She had to see people again. The first thing she needed to do was accept this party invitation. And there was no better time for a get together than Thanksgiving. Finally she had a plan, one that would fix everything.

"Come to think of it, I can't imagine anything I'd rather do. Let's get this party planned."

FARRYN PULLED THE JEEP INTO THE GARAGE AND SAT FOR A

moment preparing to enter. Mates were the sunshine of your day, the one person who made everything worthwhile, but cohabiting was hard work for a detail oriented dragon and a human whirlwind. She was under so much stress with her emerging powers that he tried not to complain, but it was driving him nuts. The worst part was her refusal to celebrate their mating with a handfasting. Did she regret it that much?

He was working on some programming for the dragon council. Their website was atrocious, and he was hired to relaunch it. In a week, his task would be done. But, he still hadn't given up hope of joining them permanently.

It was silly to bar mated dragons. Just because his powers would be bound to reduce his volatility, didn't mean he wouldn't be useful. An irritating shiver went up his spine at the thought of losing them. He wasn't looking forward to it. In his opinion, they could delay it indefinitely.

As he entered the front hallway, the delicious scent of herb roasted chicken along with Izzy's spicy orange washed over him, but he stopped dead in his tracks at the credenza. A huge pile of mail sat on it. He ground his teeth, clutter drove him nuts, and he'd asked Izzy not to leave things lying around. They had found a specific spot for everything when she moved in, and he'd move anything of his to give her more space if she needed. His new mate struggled with keeping things in their spot. It was a miracle she could find anything, ever.

This mating was harder than he expected, especially whenever his hormones kicked in, then the last thing on his mind was where she put things. He was more concerned with why she was still wearing clothes. Unfortunately, she was nowhere to be found. Her car was in the garage though.

"Izzy?"

No response. As he scooped up the mail, a gold leafed envelope caught his eye. Gold, his favorite. He had to admit, a little thrill rushed through him at the sight of it. Pulling that one from the pile, he set the rest down. It was from the council, the thrill jumped to a full on throb. What if it was an offer for a permanent position? He ripped open the envelope and gazed lovingly at the gold leaf lettering. The team had sent him an invitation to the annual Thanksgiving Beast Feast.

Unable to hold back a little dance, nothing beat winning an elusive opportunity. He couldn't wait to show this to Izzy. She probably hadn't even noticed the invitation. They needed to plan this Thanksgiving celebration to the last detail. This was his final chance to impress the team before the launch of the council's new website, the evening had to go perfectly.

Excited, he fixed his attention on the cabin, searching for any sign of his mate. His dragon ears picked up her voice out back. What was she doing outside in this weather? Good thing his DNA was running through her system from their mating, otherwise she'd get sick. He cringed at the mere thought of how vulnerable humans were, and headed toward the double doors leading onto the deck, taking a second to enjoy the view of his mate. Priceless.

Keep reading, order your copy today at
books2read.com/u/bQyXed

A NOTE FROM THE AUTHOR

Thank you for taking time out of your hectic day to read ***Dragon's Masquerade***. Making space in your mind to spend an afternoon with me was a wonderful gift. I hope you enjoyed meeting Izzy and Farryn as much as I enjoyed sharing their story. As the first couple released for public scrutiny, they will always hold a special place in my heart. If you want more, join them in ***Dragon's Feast*** where their adventure continues.

Not quite done with all the dragony goodness? Join a brand-new couple in Dragon's Second Chance. Love can be hard. Sometimes it's a winding path to that elusive Happily Ever After. Grab your copy today and revel in all the enemy to lover sauciness between Gregory and Sarah.

Dragondell VIP's get many perks, including weekly updates, extra content and giveaways. You'll also be the first to know about upcoming releases. I've been known to share some sexy shifter books for us to read together. I love reading sexy shifters, and if you do too, sign up at Bookhip.com/GTFDNL.

Now that you've reached the end of your book, please **drop everything — rush** over to your favorite bookstore and tell everyone how much you enjoyed this story. A few words on Bookbub or Goodreads would thrill me too! Reviewers are the unsung matchmakers of the reading world, helping people like us find books to love. Try it on for size, I think the job will suit you.

Welcome to Dragondell my friend, thanks again for opening your mind and letting my dragons snuggle in. Never forget I adore you, you gave my thoughts wings.

~ Dawn

ABOUT THE AUTHOR

Dawn McGraw writes paranormal shifter romance with alpha males, headstrong mates and happily ever afters. Her adventures are full of sunshine and shenanigans as humor is her go to coping method when the dark clouds of reality are closing in.

Nestled in the beautiful Rocky Mountains with her family, she counts herself a lucky Colorado native.

Connect with Dawn on her website. www.dawnmcgraw.com

facebook.com/DawnMcGrawauthorpage
twitter.com/DawnMcGrawBooks
instagram.com/dawnmcgrawbooks

www.ingramcontent.com/pod-product-compliance
Ingram Content Group UK Ltd.
Pitfield, Milton Keynes, MK11 3LW, UK
UKHW042000230426
12048UKWH00009B/452